Disney's
American Frontier #2

DAVY CROCKETT
AND THE CREEK INDIANS

Based on the Walt Disney Television Show

Written by Justine Korman
Cover Illustrated by Mike Wepplo
Illustrated by Charlie Shaw

DISNEP
PRESS
NEW YORK

FIRST EDITION
1   3   5   7   9   10   8   6   4   2

Library of Congress Catalog Card Number: 91-71357
ISBN 1-56282-005-2/1-56282-004-4 (lib. bdg.)

Consultant: Judith A. Brundin, Supervisory Education Specialist
National Museum of the American Indian
Smithsonian Institution, New York

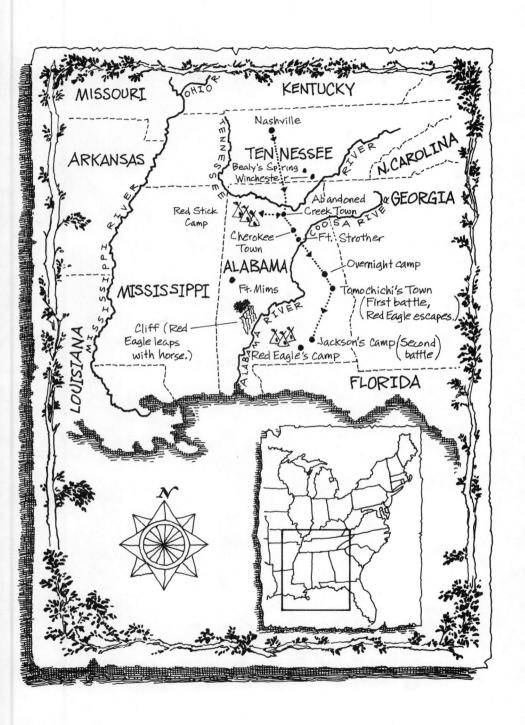

War! Rumors of battle were spreading like wildfire through the small town of Winchester, Tennessee.

Davy Crockett and his good friend Georgie Russel stood with an excited crowd in front of the courthouse, waiting for the official news. Farmers, hunters, mule drivers, carpenters, and some local Cherokee Indian people joined them.

Everyone knew that since the previous year, 1812, the British had been fighting the Americans up north, near Canada, but this latest struggle was reported to be down south, close to Tennessee. Had the British moved their forces south, or had something else happened?

A lawyer named Sam Jones climbed the courthouse steps and faced the crowd. "Gentlemen," he cried, "there has been a massacre! Five hundred people have been killed in Alabama! Not two weeks ago on August 30 in this year of our Lord, 1813, Creek Indian warriors murdered men, women, and children in Fort Mims!"

The crowd cried out in anger and disbelief. For years the Creeks had lived in peace with the settlers. Some had become farmers and others had married settlers. Why would they attack innocent people? Davy wondered. He strained forward to listen to the rest of the story.

"Frightened by rumors of an Indian uprising," Jones reported, "the settlers flocked to take Fort Mims.

"At noon on that fateful day, a band of Red Stick Creeks shot arrows tipped with fire at the fort and set it ablaze. The Creeks invaded, swinging red war clubs! Only a handful escaped the dreadful massacre that followed.

"Gentlemen," declared Jones, "we must be avenged! We must take up arms to protect our families. I will be the first to sign my name to the proud ranks of the Tennessee Volunteers! Who else will join me!"

Men rushed forward to volunteer for sixty days of service. They figured that would be plenty of time to lick the band of Creeks. They would be back in plenty of time to fill their storerooms with food for the winter ahead. Davy and Georgie stepped forward with the rest.

How'm I ever going to break this to Polly? Davy wondered, as he rode his horse the ten miles back home. She's the best wife a man could have but she raises a storm every time I go hunting for more than a week. She's like to have a hurricane over two months in the army!

Davy didn't much like the idea of war himself, but he was determined, if need be, to protect his wife and their two sons.

As Davy rode up the trail to the Crockett cabin, his sons raced to meet him. He could see Polly in the yard, hanging clothes out to dry. Polly looked up and smiled, but her smile faded when Davy told her about the war.

"I don't want you fighting," said Polly. She was frightened.

"I know," said Davy, "I don't like it any better than you do," he said. "I reckon I'd rather take orders from a polecat any day than from Ol' Hickory Face."

"Who?" Polly asked.

"General Andrew Jackson," Davy answered. "He's commanding the army. Men say he's tough as hickory wood, and that's how he got his nickname."

"The children need you more than General Jackson does," said Polly. "And so do I!"

"You're a mighty smart and pretty woman, Mrs. Crockett," Davy said. "But don't forget that the Red Stick Creeks massacred every man, woman, and child at Fort Mims. If something isn't done, they'll be in these parts next."

Polly knew Davy was right but she still didn't like it.

"I'm as able to go as any other man, and it's a duty I owe my country," said Davy. "You know my motto, Polly—"

Polly nodded. "Be sure you're right, then go ahead!"

CHAPTER 2

There were thirteen hundred Tennessee Volunteers in the camp at Bealy's Spring. Quite a few were Cherokee and Choctaw Indians. Davy had never seen so many men all in one place before.

The Volunteers elected Jones to be their captain and sent word to General Jackson that the company was assembled and ready to join him.

Captain Jones received orders that the company would move forward the following Monday. He addressed the men and gave them the opportunity to leave before then if they so desired. But each and every one of the men was determined to stay. In the busy camp, Davy recognized his neighbor John Standingdeer. They shook hands and smiled at each other.

John Standingdeer was not as tall as Davy, but he was very strong. His broad face and dark eyes were framed with straight black hair. A bright red scarf was wound like a turban around his head, and he wore a knee-length coat made from a blue trader's blanket, over buckskin leggings and moccasins.

Davy introduced John to Georgie, and the three settled comfortably under a big oak tree. Georgie passed around a jug of cider.

"John, do you know what stirred up the Creeks?" Davy asked.

"Tecumseh," John replied.

"Te-who?" Georgie asked.

"Tecumseh, Shawnee chief." John explained. "He wants to get back all the land Indians have lost to the settlers. He has a vision that the way to do this is to unite all the Indian tribes, and he has been traveling all over the country making speeches."

"But settlers bought the land from the Indians fair and square," said Georgie. "Didn't they?"

"Not all settlers were so honest," said Davy.

"That's right," said John. "Some settlers tricked tribes into agreeing to bad treaties and deals. Now some tribes have no land left at all."

"Georgie, just reckon what an awful shame that is," said Davy. "I'd hate to lose my home."

John continued. "The British got into the act, too. They told Tecumseh he could win back their land if the Indians helped the British fight the Americans. Tecumseh agreed and gathered a war party. Indian warriors are fighting alongside the British up north."

"We heard that," said Georgie.

"The British have given guns to many tribes," John went on. "They hope to have Americans fighting more than one war at once."

"Well, I heard that Tecumseh came down south here for a spell," Davy recalled. "He was asking all the tribes to fight."

"That was last autumn," said John. "While he was talking to a great council of the Creek nation, a comet flamed up in the sky. Many took it to be a sign that Tecumseh had the power of a Great Spirit."

"Folks said the same thing about that earthquake three years ago," Davy said. "They said Tecumseh stamped his foot and the earth cracked open to swallow up two towns."

"He must have pretty big feet," Georgie joked.

John laughed before he continued.

"Well, while he was down here," he said, "Tecum-seh taught the Creeks a special war dance. He gave them red war clubs and told them the clubs would protect them and drive the settlers away.

"But not all the Creeks wanted to fight. Only the Red Sticks were for war. The White Sticks were for peace."

"What're you talking about?" Georgie asked. "I thought a Creek was a Creek."

Davy shook his head. "The tribe is split into two parts."

"Each village has a White Stick chief, the Miko, and a Red Stick chief, the Tastanagi," John added.

Georgie stumbled over the unfamiliar word. "Tasta—"

"Tastanagi," Davy said. "He's a war chief. It's sort of like a general."

"Tecumseh gave all the Tastanagi bundles of sticks called Broken Days. He told them to remove one stick each day. When the sticks were gone, the attack would begin!

"There was only one Tastanagi who took Tecumseh's words to heart," John said. "Red Eagle. He led the attack on Fort Mims."

"Hold on there!" Davy said. "I've heard of Red Eagle. His daddy was a trader named Weatherford. Red Eagle's other name is Bill Weatherford."

Georgie scratched his head. "This mess gets thicker all the time. You mean the fella who stirred up this trouble isn't Indian?"

"He's half Indian," Davy said.

"Well, all's I know is he's causing misery for his kin on both sides," Georgie said. "This war is no better for Indian people than for settlers."

CHAPTER 3

The Tennessee Volunteers, in their weather-beaten buckskins and homemade backpacks, stood out among the ranks of the official army with their regulation-issue uniforms and weaponry. The Volunteers had all pretty much come as they were, with whatever weapons they had on hand. The soldiers they had joined wore crisp blue uniforms, complete with tall plumed hats. The camp had a gleaming brass cannon and stacks of rifles. General Andrew Jackson, the camp's commander, sat in his white canvas tent. He read dispatches from the other branches of his army. It was the second week of October, a month and a half since the attack on Fort Mims.

Jackson was a tall, gaunt man with a long face and fiery dark eyes. His sandy hair was shot through with gray.

As a boy, Jackson had been small and wiry. What he had lacked in size, he had made up for in toughness. He had needed to. Jackson's father had died two weeks before he was born. His two brothers were killed in the American Revolution. His mother had died shortly after, while tending to sick soldiers.

At thirteen, the orphaned Jackson had fought in the American Revolution. He was captured by a British officer. When he refused to polish the man's boots, the officer slashed the boy's hand with his saber. Jackson still carried the scar and a hatred for the British.

When Jackson first received the offer to command the Tennessee Militia from President James Madison, he was recuperating in Nashville. He had fought a duel of honor and had suffered a fractured shoulder.

Jackson was too weak even to sit up. But when he heard the news of Fort Mims, he cried, "By the Eternal, these people must be avenged!"

In just nine days Jackson's army was on its way. The men marched south through thick woods. Jackson drove them at the hard pace of twenty miles a day. The men respected their stern leader and knew he suffered as much as any of them.

Jackson forced his mind away from the pain in his shoulder to study the dispatches.

The American army was closing in on the Red Stick Creeks from three directions. There was the Georgia Militia and Creek Indian White Sticks coming from the east. A federal army with a Choctaw company was headed up from the south. From the north marched

Jackson's own Tennessee militia with six hundred Cherokees.

Jackson put down the papers. He looked out his tent across the broad Tennessee River. Somewhere out there under the bright fall trees were Red Eagle and his warriors. But where?

Jackson called out to his aide, "Where's that scout I told you to find, Major Norton?"

Norton trotted into the tent. He trembled before the general. "They say the best man is one of the Volunteers . . . uh, name of Crockett."

Major Norton was short, with a round face and neat sideburns. His new blue uniform was trimmed with bright gold braid and a pair of gleaming epaulets. His boots were brightly polished.

Ever since his run-in with that British officer, Jackson had hated the sight of polished boots.

"Well, where is he?" Jackson demanded.

"As a matter of fact, General, he's out hunting," Norton said. "We're short on rations. He's gone across the river to the woods."

"That's enemy territory!" Jackson exclaimed. "Rations aren't what you're short on, it's brains! If that man starts shooting all over the woods he'll draw every Red Stick for a hundred miles."

"He didn't take a gun, sir," Norton said, hoping to calm his commander.

"That's the most ridiculous thing I've ever heard! How can he hunt with no gun?" Jackson demanded.

"I . . . don't know, sir," Norton replied.

"By the Eternal!" Jackson sputtered. "I want this Crockett fellow and I want him right now! Fetch him!"

Norton shivered and saluted with a shaking hand. "Yes, sir!"

On the other side of the Tennessee River, Davy and Georgie tracked a bear into a thicket.

"Mighty big one, Davy," Georgie whispered.

"Yeah, he sure is," Davy agreed, in a hushed voice.

"Now's a good time to try out that idea I was telling you about."

"Well, give that old grin everything you've got," Georgie said.

Carrying only his knife, Davy strolled into the thicket. The bear growled.

Georgie leaned against a sycamore tree to wait. He didn't see Major Norton and two soldiers awkwardly paddling toward them in a canoe. But he heard them all right.

"Crockett!" Norton was shouting. The canoe pulled up onto the grassy bank. As the men walked, twigs creaked and leaves rustled.

Georgie waved for quiet. But when the major saw him, he ignored him and cried even louder, "Crockett!"

Georgie pointed to the thicket. He kept trying to hush the noisy major.

"Crockett's in there?" Norton asked impatiently. He glared at Georgie.

"He's trying to grin down a bear," Georgie explained.

"Grin down a . . . you backwoods buffoons think the rest of us will believe anything, don't you?" Norton said. He shouted into the thicket. "Crockett, can't you hear me?"

The bear bellowed. Davy came tumbling out of the bushes in a hurry.

"You sure spoiled things good," he scolded Norton. "Now I've got to do it the old-fashioned way." Davy plunged back into the thicket, brandishing his knife.

"Yahoo! Give him what for, Davy!" Georgie cried, waving his hat in the air.

The bushes shook and swayed as if a hurricane were wrestling a tornado. The bear roared like thunder. Davy made no sound at all.

Then Davy fell out of the bushes again. Georgie caught him and pushed him back in.

"Stick with him, Davy!" Georgie cried.

Norton's jaw dropped. He could hardly believe his eyes.

The bushes were still. All was silent. Then Davy emerged, wiping his knife. He studied Major Norton's pale face and crisp uniform. His brass belt buckle, epaulets, and shiny boots were bright enough to blind a

man. Why doesn't he just stand on a hilltop and holler, Here I am! Davy thought.

"Now, Major, you wanted to see me?" Davy asked.

"Ge . . . Ge . . . General Jackson wants to see you," Norton stammered. He stared at the tall man in the coonskin cap.

"We'll be along directly," Davy said.

"Just as soon as we get that ol' bear poled up." Davy turned to the major's escort. "C'mon, boys! Give us a hand. It's a fair-to-middling size critter."

Norton's escort carried the huge bear on a pole through the army camp. The hungry soldiers waved and cheered.

"Full bellies tonight, boys!" Davy cried. He strolled through camp on his way to Jackson's tent.

"Hear you want to see me, General," Davy told the commander.

"That's right, come inside," Jackson said. He lifted the canvas flap. "That's the largest bear I've seen in a long time. How did you kill it?"

"With my knife," Davy answered. "I was figuring on grinning him to death. But this stumble-footed major of yours busted up my concentrating."

"Grinning him to death? What in thunderation is that?" Jackson wondered.

"Oh, it's something I've been experimenting with," Davy explained. "You see there's nothing so irresistible as an old-fashioned, good-natured grin. Like this."

Davy flashed his biggest grin. "I started out on raccoons. I got so good at it, one day an old raccoon threw up his hands the minute he saw my teeth and said, 'Ya got me, Davy!' And he scrambled down the tree he was in and plopped himself in my sack before I could blink."

The general smiled. This Crockett was his kind of man.

Davy grinned. He loved telling tall tales, the taller the better. Every time he told this one, the story just got better.

Norton scowled. How could Jackson tolerate this rude, unshaven bumpkin in greasy buckskins? The man looked as if he'd never even seen a bar of soap, much less used one.

"I figured the same thing ought to work on bears. But I didn't get the chance to find out," Davy continued. "I wound up having to wrestle this particular critter into table meat. What were you hankering to see me about, General?"

"We're on the edge of hostile territory," Jackson told him. He was serious again. "I want a scouting party to find out what the Red Sticks are up to. Are you willing to volunteer?"

"I reckon Georgie and I will be glad to get out of camp for a spell," Davy answered.

Jackson frowned. "This is a military operation, not a hunting frolic. Major Norton and an army squad will accompany you."

"That won't make the chore easier, General," Davy said. "Like you say, hunting Creek warriors in their own country is no frolic. There's no room for green-horns."

Crockett was afraid that Major Norton would accidentally give them away. He didn't want to get caught by the Red Stick Creeks just because Norton stepped on a twig.

"You know the woods, Crockett. My men will go with you. Just be sure the major brings back the information I want," the general said.

Davy still didn't like the idea of tracking with extra company. But orders were orders and he was in the army now.

"Come on, Major," Davy said. He left the general's tent.

Norton hastily saluted the general and then followed Davy.

CHAPTER 4

Davy and Georgie rode with Major Norton at the head of the scouting party. John Standingdeer and a Choctaw named Mosholatubbee were along as were eight cavalry soldiers called dragoons. The party splashed across the Tennessee River and worked its way into the woods.

John and Mosholatubbee were sent ahead as advance scouts. The Indians could "read" the woods even better than Davy could. They could also be as silent and invisible as the Red Stick men. And if they were caught, they might be able to convince the Red Stick warriors that they were just hunting.

Despite Davy's warning to be quiet, Major Norton chattered noisily the whole way. Davy could tell that the man was nervous and inexperienced and tried to hide this by attempting to sound tough.

"Indians are simpleminded savages," Norton as-serted. "The only thing they understand is a musket-ball."

Davy winced at the word *savages*. Most Indians he'd known were a lot more civilized than Major Norton.

"Well the best warrior among them isn't really Indian," Davy said. "Red Eagle's other name is Bill Weatherford. His father was a Scottish trader. His uncle Alexander McGillivray was a general in the Revolution."

"That explains his superior cunning," Norton sniffed.

"And his bloodthirstiness," Davy snapped back. "Most Creek warriors won't kill the way Red Eagle did at Fort Mims. Instead, they fight in small parties, maybe thirty or forty men, and then only long enough to draw first blood. Afterward they go home for a big dance and a feast."

"Sounds civilized to me," Georgie said.

"Indian warriors fight for honor," Davy said. Davy couldn't help trying to educate Major Norton. It was men like Norton, with their lack of understanding, who often caused wars, Davy thought.

It had been a tiring day of trailblazing. During the last hour of daylight, Davy dismounted one more time to look for Red Stick tracks.

John Standingdeer and Mosholatubbee rejoined the main party. They had covered a lot of ground but had seen no sign of the Creeks.

"You've done nothing but lead us through swamps, canebrakes, and briar patches all day," Norton complained. "Soon it will be nightfall. I see a trail over there and there's no reason not to take it."

"There's plenty reason not to take it if you want to go on breathing!" Davy said.

John nodded. "The Red Sticks would watch that trail."

"When I want advice I'll ask for it!" Norton fumed. "We'll cover more ground if we separate. I'm taking that trail. We'll meet back here in this clearing by dawn."

"Maybe you and Mosholatubbee had best stay with the major and see that he doesn't get into too much trouble," Davy suggested to John.

Norton turned beet red, but kept silent for once.

"I'll do my best," John promised.

"Good luck, Major," said Davy. "We'd better fix up a signal in case either of us finds Red Stick tracks. Let's use an animal call, so we don't tip off Red Eagle. Can you do a hoot owl?"

"Certainly," Norton replied. He cupped his hand over his mouth and hooted. It was pretty comical to watch the dignified major hoot like an owl. His soldiers laughed.

Norton signaled his men to move out. Davy and Georgie watched their bright uniforms move between the branches ablaze with autumn·foliage.

The orange moon rose fat and full above the hills. Davy and Georgie tied their horses and climbed a hill. They wanted to see the lay of the land from above.

Davy and Georgie looked grim as they stared down. There was a large band of Creek men. They were almost close enough to reach out and touch the warriors padding single file between red-leafed oaks. War parties usually traveled this way, stepping in each other's footprints to confuse enemies. A single-file trail made it impossible to tell how many braves there were.

Davy and Georgie crouched behind some bushes hoping none of the warriors would look their way. It wouldn't do to get caught now!

Suddenly a deer sprang past where they were hiding. It bounded downhill, its white tail flashing. Davy looked up to see what had scared it and saw a second party of Red Stick Creeks coming over the crest of the hill.

Davy and Georgie burrowed deeper into the thicket. Through a screen of leaves, they watched the painted warriors approach.

Davy recognized the young Tastanagi in the lead. His face, neck, and shoulders were painted red.

"That's Red Eagle," Davy whispered.

The war chief was followed by a silent line of Red Stick braves. Bright red stripes blazed like blood on their dark faces. Their heads were shaved on the sides so their black hair grew in a stiff crest of bristles. Small braids dangled from their foreheads and down the back of their necks. Many of the men wore shell rings in their ears. They also wore buckskins and wide belts beaded with porcupine quills.

"Sure are a lot of 'em," Davy whispered.

Most of the braves clutched tomahawks and wooden war clubs, spears, hickory bows, and cane arrows. Many had sharp cane knives stuck in their belt.

A few toted long rifles like Davy's, but decorated with beads and feathers. Many were of British make.

Davy and Georgie waited until the last Red Stick vanished into the woods below.

"How many did you count?" Georgie asked.

"About sixty," Davy said. "Let's follow them to their camp and see how many there are all together."

Davy and Georgie silently followed in the Indians' footsteps and again climbed a rocky cliff to look down on the scene below. There was the Red Stick camp. Georgie gasped. The camp was swarming with warriors stamping out a dance to the beat of drums.

"There must be hundreds!" Georgie said. "Maybe thousands."

"I've never seen so many," Davy said. "Looks like Red Eagle's talked the rest of his tribe into following him. We'd best get back to the major."

Davy and Georgie hurried as fast as they dared back through the moonlit woods. Under the full moon it was almost as easy as traveling by day. They arrived at the

clearing and quickly hid, watching and waiting. The moon rose higher in the clear, black sky. They heard the shrill scream of a bobcat somewhere in the woods. Crickets chirped and creaked in the dark.

Finally Davy heard an owl call. He hooted his reply. He heard an answering hoot and he and Georgie got on their horses and followed the sound.

Georgie pointed to a bare sycamore branch. Davy saw an old gray owl blinking his big yellow eyes.

The two friends smiled. They'd been fooled by a real owl! Then their smiles faded. "Where's Norton?" they wondered, worried.

Distant gunfire shattered the night. The owl flapped away.

"Sounds like the major got himself in trouble," Georgie said. He and Davy rode back toward the river and the sounds of battle.

They watched Norton and his dragoons fire from under cover on the riverbank. They had been ambushed while trying to get across.

The Red Sticks fired arrows from their hideout in the boulders of the cliffs overhanging the water. Arrows whistled one way through the night. Guns flashed and roared the other way, the echoes of the shots mingling with shrill Indian war cries.

"I suppose we'll have to save him," said Davy.

"How?" Georgie wondered.

"We'll give them the old Crockett charge!" said Davy.

They got on their horses and galloped to the rescue.

A swift arrow thunked into a tree trunk beside Major Norton's head. The frightened officer was out of ammunition and about to give up hope. Suddenly the rocks rang with echoing shouts and hoofbeats.

"Brigade halt!"

"Company halt!"

"Company B, forward march!"

"Brigade charge!"

"Company charge!"

"It's the general and the whole regiment!" Norton said, excitedly—and with relief.

The soldiers cheered. Now it was the Red Sticks' turn to panic. In the echoing darkness, it sounded like a huge army was bearing down on them.

"Dragoons dismount!" a loud voice commanded. "On the double now. Fire at will. Charge!"

"Company B, close up!" another voice shouted from the opposite side.

Convinced they were outnumbered, the Red Sticks backed away, still firing. Once they were out of sight, Norton looked around him. He was quite surprised to see the "reinforcements" emerge from the dark bushes.

"Company A reporting," Davy saluted.

Georgie slipped out of the underbrush. "Company B reporting, Major."

"You mean . . . just the two of you?" Norton asked, astonished.

"Don't forget our horses," Georgie said. "Left them back in the bushes with orders to stamp their hearts out."

"You drove away all those Red Sticks!" Norton was still amazed.

"They were just a little war party, anyway," Davy told him.

"Yeah," Georgie agreed. He pointed to the ridge. "The whole Creek nation is gathering up there."

"Take care of your casualties," Davy told Norton. "Georgie and I will take the news back to the general as soon as we can catch our horses."

CHAPTER 5

oosters crowed at the rising red sun when Davy and Georgie rode into camp. Davy pushed past a sleepy sentry in front of General Jackson's tent.

"The general's expecting me," Davy explained, lifting the tent flap. "Sorry to disturb you, General."

Jackson sat up on his cot, instantly alert. "Never mind. What did you find out?"

"Well, they aim to fight. They were holding a war dance last night. Their camp is back in the mountains, about ten or twenty miles from where we crossed the river," Davy reported.

"How many?" Jackson asked.

"Plenty, and they're still coming in," Davy replied. "Red Eagle is there."

"Where's Major Norton?" Jackson wanted to know.

"Oh, he had a little trouble," Davy explained. "He'll be along directly."

Jackson knew he had to act quickly. He called his sentry and gave orders to rouse the camp. "We're moving out!"

"Sure do admire a man who doesn't do his fighting on the seat of his britches, General," Davy said.

Eight hundred Volunteers forded the cold waters of the Tennessee River at a shallow point nearly two miles across. The rough, creviced river bottom cruelly jolted the men, who were already cold and tired. Many of their horses had to be left behind when their hooves became stuck in the treacherous rocky crevices. The crossing was an awful experience.

Things did not fare much better for the men once they were on the other side of the river. Their rations were almost gone, and they were living on parched corn. The dried kernels could be mixed with water to make hard biscuits or lumpy porridge. Or it could be eaten plain. A man could live on parched corn, but it was hardly tasty.

Davy approached Major Norton.

"Major, the men are powerful hungry. I calculate I could rustle up some grub if you would be good enough to let me do a little shooting while we march," Davy said. This time he would not use his knife or try grinning his game to death. The situation called for quick killing.

Norton frowned. "A rifle shot might rouse the enemy. They would surely come to investigate."

"Hunger's a mighty fierce enemy and he's already here," Davy argued.

The major looked thoughtful. "Well, you have a point. Very well, then. But be careful."

"Much obliged," Davy said. He and Georgie soon set out in search of game. They would ride ahead of the marching army.

Not far from the headwaters of the river, Davy and Georgie came to the edge of the woods. They had not seen so much as a field mouse and were feeling mighty discouraged.

"With all the warriors and soldiers in these parts I reckon the critters are plumb hunted out," Davy said.

Georgie agreed. "What hasn't been shot's been scared away."

They were facing a huge cornfield, drily rattling in the brisk breeze off the river. Several dugout canoes lay on the bank. On the other side of the field stood the log buildings of a Creek town.

Davy signaled Georgie for quiet. They did not know if this was the village of a friendly tribe.

There seemed to be no smoking fires or any other signs of life. Then Davy found fresh Indian tracks among the row of withered cornstalks.

"Reckon they heard us coming," Davy said.

"Maybe they're fixin' to ambush us," Georgie said. He glanced warily over his shoulder.

"Best get back to our brigade," Davy suggested. Just then a noisy column of soldiers marched along the trail into the field. The army had caught up with its hunting scouts.

Major Norton was curious about the eerily quiet town. "Why would they just abandon their homes?"

"Would you want a war in your backyard?" Davy replied. "Reckon they just don't want to get mixed up in this mess."

"I'm not so sure," Norton said. "This could be a trap. But if it is empty, then perhaps they left some food behind. We shall commandeer their supplies."

Major Norton sent Davy, Georgie and John off with a small squad to search the empty village for food. Davy and the others eased down the streets of the village, ever on the alert.

The party spread out into the surrounding huts where the villagers lived. The log and thatch houses were arranged in groups of four. Each group belonged to one family. Some houses had walls woven of split saplings covered with thick clay. Others were built of logs, much like Davy's home.

The soldiers crept toward each cluster of houses. They pointed their rifles inside the dark doorways. Their hearts pounded—a fierce warrior might be hiding inside. But they found no one.

John pointed to small round huts on spindly stilts.

"Those are the granaries," he said. The granaries

stood at the ends of small gardens bordering each family's cluster of huts.

There was a notched-log ladder leading up to each granary door. Davy climbed up one and found a few baskets of multicolored corn inside. There were also baskets of dried beans, pumpkins, and squash. But not a lot.

None of the others found much food, either. They gathered all they could and returned to Norton and the waiting troops.

The food didn't last long. Seemed like in the wink of an eye all the men were hungry again.

Soon Davy and Georgie set out once more to hunt. They hadn't been walking long when a large pack of hogs came snorting through a stand of oaks.

Davy quickly loaded his rifle, sighted down the long barrel, and squeezed the trigger. A large hog dropped in its tracks. The others ran squealing toward the camp.

In a few minutes, the soldiers' guns roared as if war had broken out. Davy shouldered the fat hog he had shot. When he got back to camp, he found the soldiers had killed the other hogs and a stray cow.

"You know, Major, cows and hogs don't roam wild in these parts," Davy told Norton. "These critters must belong to somebody."

"They probably ran away from that village we saw," Norton said.

"All I know is we can sure use the food."

*　　*　　*

The next morning, the Volunteers marched into a Cherokee town. The town's friendly chief, Pathkiller, greeted them.

"Howdy!" the chief called.

Pathkiller's head was wrapped in a colorful cloth turban. Under his tunic made of traders' blankets was a white shirt and silk cravat. Fringed leggings covered the tops of his moccasins.

His clothes combined styles of both Indian and settler dress. That meant Pathkiller's people often traded with settlers.

"Have you seen any warriors?" Davy asked him.

"Red Eagle and his warriors just passed through town," Pathkiller told them. He looked troubled. "Red Eagle vowed to return and destroy any tribes who refuse to join his cause."

"The army will protect all peaceful tribes!" Norton declared.

Pathkiller was not so sure. These soldiers looked scrawny and tired. Red Eagle's men had been fierce and well fed.

"I am sure you are all very brave," Pathkiller said. "And perhaps hungry as well. We would offer you meat, but our pigs and cows are missing."

The men exchanged guilty glances.

"Reckon Uncle Sam ought to repay these good folks," Davy told Major Norton.

*　　*　　*

The men returned to camp tired and hungry and had no trouble falling asleep that night. But the quiet camp was roused at midnight when an Indian messenger came running, shouting, "Captain Jackson!"

CHAPTER
6

The messenger, a White Stick chief named Tomochichi, had run a great distance to reach Jackson's camp at Fort Strother.

"Red Eagle knows you are here," he told General Jackson. "His spies have followed your army. He told us Sharpknife was coming with many fine horses, blankets, and guns."

Jackson looked confused. "Sharpknife?"

"That is your Indian name," Tomochichi explained.

"The Red Sticks have surrounded our village. If we help them fight you, Red Eagle has promised us a share of the spoils. But if we don't, they have vowed to take our weapons and food."

"What did you tell Red Eagle?" Jackson asked.

"Our council asked for three days to consider his offer. If at the end of that time we do not join the fight, we will give the Red Sticks our village to avoid bloodshed," Tomochichi replied.

"When did this happen?" Jackson asked.

"Very early this morning," Tomochichi said. "Before sunrise I dressed in a hog skin and rooted and grunted past the Red Stick camp to bring you this news."

"You won't lose your town, Chief," Jackson assured him. He clasped Tomochichi's forearm in the Creek fashion. Then he sprang into action.

"Norton! My horse!" Jackson cried. "Wake the men and saddle the horses—we're moving out!"

Two soldiers helped the ailing general mount his horse. He winced at the pain in his shoulder.

In an hour the army was crossing the Coosa River. They traveled the rest of the night and part of the next day through thick forest. They finally stopped to rest six miles from Tomochichi's town.

The tired, hungry troops slept. Jackson propped himself against a tree trunk and listened to reports from his scouts until daybreak.

An hour after sunrise, the sleepless general led his army forward again. Soon they reached a ridge overlooking the town. It was surrounded by a log wall and sat cradled in the loop of a creek.

Davy climbed the ridge to stand near the general. Despite his injury, Jackson cut a fine figure in his blue coat and big black crescent-shaped hat. His tasseled sword gleamed in the bright morning sun. On his left stood a young bugler in a red coat with yellow braid. A standard-bearer held Old Glory snapping in the brisk breeze.

"We can't find hide nor hair of Red Eagle and his boys," Davy reported. "They're probably holed up real good just waiting for us to make the first move."

Jackson nodded in agreement.

"When we catch Red Eagle, this war will be over," Jackson said. "We'll draw him out. There's only two ways out of there, and I've got them both covered. Company A will block one way and Company B the other.

"As soon as the soldiers are positioned, you Volunteers jump in there and draw those Red Sticks out of hiding. We can fight them better once we can see them!"

"I sure hope your sharpshooters don't mistake *us* for Indians," Davy said.

"If they do I'll see they apologize," Jackson joked.

Davy, Georgie, and a party of rangers carefully picked their way down the face of the ridge. The rangers moved from cover to cover as quietly as they could through dry brush and fallen leaves.

Once the rangers were in sight of the town's log walls, the White Sticks began to shout friendly greetings, designed to be heard by the Red Sticks.

"Howdy, Brother, Howdy!" the White Sticks yelled. They pointed toward the tree-fringed creek, where Davy could see war-painted faces, gleaming tomahawks, and the muzzles of muskets poking out from the bushes.

Shots suddenly roared from the Red Sticks' hiding place, shattering the morning silence. Echoes rolled like thunder through the hills.

Davy and the rangers returned fire. Then they retreated to reload and to draw the Red Sticks farther out in the open. The Red Sticks shot off arrows as they advanced, until they were close enough to shoot their rifles. The rangers fired back and retreated once more. Just as Jackson had hoped, the Red Sticks followed. Suddenly they found themselves face to face with Company A! The soldiers discharged their muskets with a thunderous roar. The startled Red Sticks scattered through the trees.

A second heavy volley of bullets from the soldiers hit the Red Sticks. They turned and headed in a new direction.

But now they faced Company B! The warriors were trapped between the two lines of soldiers. At Norton's command, Company B emptied their muskets with a deafening blast.

Between the two lines, warriors and soldiers were locked in hand-to-hand combat. Whoops and battle cries rang out among flashing tomahawks and slashing bayonets. Officers screamed orders amid the chaos. The groaning wounded fell to the dead leaves at the feet of the fighting men.

Red Eagle charged a ranger. The red-painted chief smashed his heavy war club into the man's side. Then he whirled to face Davy, who ducked as the chief waved the war club again. Davy rushed at Red Eagle's middle and wrestled him to the ground. The two fought and tumbled over the crackling leaves.

Red Eagle rolled against a fallen horse. Davy struggled to keep him pinned and, at the same time, to reach for his hunting knife.

Another Red Stick, seeing his Tastanagi in trouble, quickly threw a rock. It hit Davy on the forehead, and he dropped to the ground, out cold.

Red Eagle raised his tomahawk. Georgie spied Davy and Red Eagle through a tangle of clashing bayonets and tomahawks. He quickly lifted his rifle and shot the tomahawk from the startled chief's hand. Weaponless, Red Eagle retreated.

Georgie rushed to Davy's side and examined a wound on his head. To Georgie's relief, Davy wasn't badly hurt.

Realizing that they had been trapped and being very low on weapons, Red Eagle rallied his warriors to try a daring plan.

The Red Sticks charged Company B. Just as Norton's men raised their rifles and fired, the Red Sticks dropped to the ground.

The bullets whizzed harmlessly over the Creeks'

heads. They rained down on the dry leaves, rattling like hail.

Norton's men stopped to reload and the Red Sticks leaped right over them! One warrior slashed out at Norton with his tomahawk. The major tried to duck, but feared his hour had come.

Then the wind whistled with a swift arrow. The warrior fell dead at Norton's feet.

John Standingdeer nodded gravely to Norton. The major gave his thanks in a quavering voice.

Norton looked for Red Eagle. But the chief and his warriors had already vanished into the mountains.

"I reckon Red Eagle's tomahawk has an awful nick in it," Georgie said. He dabbed Davy's bloody forehead with his handkerchief.

"Got away, did he?" Davy asked, dazed.

"Yeah, but a lot of them didn't."

Back at Fort Strother, Jackson fumed.

"Don't call it a victory around me, Major."

"Their casualties were enormous compared to ours," Norton argued. "We captured three Red Stick chiefs who are anxious to discuss terms for peace."

"Peace! Thunderation, Norton! How can you talk about peace with Red Eagle and most of his band still on the loose?" Jackson raged. He paced his tent.

"We'll have him in short order, Sir," Norton as-serted. He waved a sheaf of dispatches. "There are Georgia Volunteers on the way. The 39th Infantry is coming up from the south. And three hundred White Stick Creeks have joined us. The Red Sticks don't have a chance against such an army!"

Jackson crumpled the papers. He thrust his red face in Norton's.

"Taking after Red Eagle will be like trying to run down a fox in a briar patch," Jackson thundered. "There are hundreds of miles of woods too thick to march through. We'll never find him in all that land!"

CHAPTER 7

It was two weeks before Christmas and the camp was covered in snow. Inside his tent General Jackson was reading a letter from Tennessee governor William Blount to his officers. Jackson was still weak from his wounded shoulder. He and his officers were freezing cold and badly in need of food.

"Governor Blount advises evacuation of the fortress and retreat." Jackson finished the letter. Clearly he did not like the idea.

Norton shook his head. "Retreat? Never!"

"Maybe the governor is right," Colonel Coffee said. The commander of the cavalry was a practical man. He had the courage to say what was on the minds of several other officers.

"The men are hungry, cold, and discouraged. Many are refusing to take orders. Their terms of service are up. We can't hold them here. And we can't fight a war without supplies, General," Coffee said.

"We might be facing a mutiny," agreed Captain Reid.

"Perhaps we should regroup and come back later with fresh supplies and new volunteers," Major Ridge suggested.

"We will not stop until Red Eagle is in chains!" Jackson stormed.

Just then, Davy lifted the tent flap. A fresh, frigid gust of wind blew in as Davy and Georgie stepped inside.

"Excuse me, General," Davy said.

"Well, what do you want?" Jackson demanded.

"Nothing much. Just dropped in to say good-bye," said Davy.

"Good-bye! Where do you think you're going?" Jackson thundered.

"Home. You see, General, we only volunteered for sixty days and that's long since up. We've served our term and then some. Catching Red Eagle is liable to take up the rest of the year."

The officers exchanged worried glances. If the Volunteers left, there would be no chance of winning. Jackson had to convince them to stay!

"You're going after Red Eagle with the rest of the troops. This war isn't over yet," the general stated in his firmest voice.

"Well, we aren't quitting," Davy explained. "My neighbors and I will be back directly. We have to see that our families have food for the winter before we come back, and I need some warm clothes and a fresh horse. My stallion's plumb tuckered out, and he sure could use some Tennessee oats."

Jackson frowned. Crockett didn't seem to understand the nature of military orders.

Davy frowned, too. Jackson didn't seem to understand that the Volunteers were here to protect their families. If their families had no food for the winter, then they weren't being protected very well.

"Desertion is a serious crime in the army, Crockett," Norton chimed in.

"How can it be desertion if we've served our term?" Georgie shouted.

"Besides, I just told you we were coming back," Davy added.

"You're confined to this camp. That's an order," Norton blustered.

Davy shook his head. "I promised my family I'd be home in sixty days and I'm late already. A promise is a promise." He turned to Jackson. "Sorry, General," he added.

Davy and Georgie left the tent. Norton said to Jackson, "If he's permitted to leave it will destroy the discipline of the whole camp."

"He's attached to *your* command, Major," Jackson angrily reminded Norton. "And Crockett isn't the only one who wants to go home. We have another brigade of

Volunteers, from east Tennessee, more than a thousand men whose time is up," said the general.

"That'll leave us with only five hundred men," Norton concluded. "And most of those are due to go home soon, too. Only Colonel Coffee's cavalry will stay."

"I can't run a war with one hundred and thirty cavalry!" Jackson boomed.

"I'll stop Crockett!" Norton cried.

"Halt!" Major Norton yelled, raising his hand. He stood on the bridge between Davy and the road home. A gunner beside Norton held a lighted match above the touchhole of a cannon. Army regulars were strung along on both sides of the bridge arching over the icy creek.

"Sure got his back up," Georgie observed.

Davy rode slowly across the bridge. When he got up to the cannon, he advised the gunner, "Careful, don't burn yourself."

The gunner shook out his match and grinned. "Bring us some bear meat when you come back, Davy."

"By the Eternal!" shouted a harsh voice.

Jackson galloped up on his horse. Colonel Coffee rode his dappled gray stallion beside Jackson. The loyal cavalry followed.

Jackson rode straight through the ranks of home-bound Volunteers, and snatched a musket from one of them. He cradled the gun in his good arm and leveled it across his horse's neck.

"I'll shoot the first man who deserts!" Jackson warned, blocking the bridge.

"Save your bullets for Red Eagle," Davy said. "Besides, that musket's rusted solid."

For a long moment the only sound was the wind whistling through the bare tree branches and the snorting of restless horses. Then Jackson slowly lowered his eyes to take a closer look at the rifle. He threw it on the ground. His blue eyes blazed with fury. Davy and the men marched on.

Davy and Georgie had smelled wood smoke in the cold air for quite a while. Davy knew they were near his cabin. They rounded one last snowy hill and saw the smoking chimney of home amid bare trees. Davy's eyes filled with joy as he watched his sons run up the snowy patch.

"Daddy's home!" the boys shrieked. Polly came rushing out to greet Davy. She hugged her husband.

She was so happy she even hugged Georgie. Georgie squirmed free of her embrace, shy as a schoolboy. He blushed.

"You're never going to get a wife that way," Davy teased. He took Polly in his arms and gave her a long kiss.

Billy and Johnny covered their eyes.

"Sure is a lot of kissing whenever Daddy comes home," Johnny complained.

"Ugh, mush!" agreed Billy.

Davy discovered he'd come home just in time. The larder was empty. The woodpile had vanished.

When Davy reckoned he chopped about enough firewood, he determined to set out hunting. "I am mighty tired of parched corn," he told his family. "I aim to rustle up a regular feast."

"You missed all the good bear hunting," Billy said.

"They were fat and plenty," Johnny agreed.

Davy shook his head sadly. He knew a fat bear was easily taken because it can't run fast or for long. He was sorry he'd been too busy fighting Indians to bag a nice plump bear for Christmas dinner.

"Reckon we'll have to settle for some gobblers," Davy said.

Billy asked eagerly, "Can I come along, Dad? Can I?"

"Well . . ." Davy hesitated. His brown eyes twinkled with mischief. "I suppose—"

"Yippee!" Billy hollered.

Davy patted little Johnny's head. "You'll be old enough soon. You stay here and take care of your momma while Billy and I are gone."

Davy and Billy put on woolen wrappers and fresh moccasins. They stuffed the toes of the moccasins with moss for warmth.

Davy refilled his powder horn and pouch of musket balls. He stuck his big hunting knife and a tomahawk through his belt and hung a bag of coarse salt over his shoulder. If the hunt was successful, they would need the salt to preserve the meat until they got home.

The two hunters stepped out of the cozy cabin. The wind howled through the bare trees. The sky was heavy with gray clouds. A few snowflakes swirled in the breeze.

Davy whistled for his dogs. Bullet, Whirlwind, and Blue came running. The hounds barked joyously, their breath puffing like clouds in the cold air.

Davy and Billy headed for the frozen woods. The eager dogs bounded ahead, leaving tracks in the snow.

It started to snow hard and then to sleet.

"Weather like this makes the going mighty rough," Davy said. "But it usually means good hunting."

Soon the dogs startled a large group of turkeys. Davy and Billy shot one big bird apiece. The Crocketts rested beneath a big oak tree, its branches heavy with snow.

Blue sniffed a fallen log. He raised his face to the gray sky and howled. Then off he went with Whirlwind and Bullet close behind.

Davy followed the dogs as fast as he could. Billy kept up, despite the stinging sleet. But the baying dogs were soon out of sight. They vanished behind a curtain of icy sleet.

Davy could hear the hounds howling. He followed the sound. His muscles strained against leggings stiff with ice. The wet turkeys bounced heavily on his shoulders.

When Davy and Billy reached the dogs, they were barking up an empty tree.

"Must've been a turkey that flew away," Davy told his son.

"Maybe it's a bear!" Billy exclaimed.

"Bears are rare this time of year. They take to house when it's this cold," Davy explained. "They get very fat in the fall and early part of the winter. Then they go into holes in large hollow trees or logs and sleep there clear through 'til spring."

The dogs took off again. Davy and his son followed. This time they found the hounds circling an elm.

"They're barking up the wrong tree again!" Davy said. There was nothing in the tree but ice.

The dogs led the Crocketts on a chase through the frozen trees. Whirlwind, Bullet, and Blue stopped three or four times at empty trees.

"I don't know what's wrong with these hounds," Davy said. "But if they don't stop this wild goose chase, we'll have hound dog for Christmas dinner!"

Then he reached a large, black oak. When Davy took a closer look and saw deep claw marks on the bark, he knew that a bear had been in the tree.

"You're right, Billy! There is a bear!" Davy said. He pointed to the claw marks. "When they climb up a tree, bears don't slip. But as they come down, they make long scratches with their nails. One just climbed down."

Just then the dogs barked furiously. The Crocketts crept to the edge of an open prairie. The dogs had cornered a huge black bear against a rocky bluff.

"That's the biggest bear I ever seen!" Davy declared.

"He sure is," Billy said, in awe.

The bear opened his enormous jaws and let loose an earsplitting roar. The dogs backed away, but kept barking.

Davy took the turkeys from his back and hung them on a sapling.

"The hounds were afraid to attack him. That's why they stopped so often," Davy told Billy.

The bear roared again. The dogs backed up farther. Fearful whines mixed with their barks.

The bear charged, raking his claws. His powerful jaws swung from side to side. The dogs plunged into bare bushes. With his path clear, the bear bounded away.

Soon Davy saw the bear not far away, climbing up a fat elm tree. The dogs barked and bayed. The bear sat in the fork of the tree and growled at them.

Davy dropped to the snow. He crawled till he was within eighty yards of the bear, and then he fired. The shot echoed through the woods. Snow fell from branches. The bear raised a paw and snorted loudly.

Davy couldn't tell if he'd hit his mark. He loaded his gun again as quickly as he could. At the next shot, the bear came tumbling down.

"I calculate that varmint must weigh six hundred

pounds," Davy told his grinning boy. "We can't wrastle him home ourselves. Have to come back with help."

They skinned and butchered the bear, separating the fat from the meat. They salted the meat and put it on a rough scaffold they had rigged high up in the tree branches. This would keep the meat safe from wolves.

Billy and Davy blazed a trail home, slicing strips of bark off trees to mark their path until they reached the woods near their cabin.

With a neighbor's help, and four horses, Davy and Billy brought back the bear. They shared the meat with their neighbor, and still had plenty left for Polly's pantry.

Later, in front of the fireplace, Polly said, "I sure missed you an awful lot."

Davy said, "I missed you, too."

"The younguns like to pester me to death. Hasn't been a morning since you went away they haven't said, 'Maybe Pa will be home today.' But thank the Lord, you're home for good."

"Well, not exactly," Davy said reluctantly. "The war is not quite over yet."

"You're going back?" Polly asked.

"Now don't take on. I had enough trouble with the army over coming home. My major and I didn't quite see eye to eye on that. But I figured I was right, and you know me. When I'm sure I'm right, I go ahead! Nothing could be more right than this."

Polly sighed.

By Christmas Day the weather had cleared. The Crocketts had a grand dinner with roast turkey, bear, fresh-baked cornbread, and pudding.

As they sat around the table, the Crocketts heard the distant booming of their neighbors' guns. Shooting a salute on Christmas Day was a popular custom.

"It's time for the Christmas salute!" Davy told his sons.

The boys cheered. The Crocketts put on warm clothes and went outside. Davy loaded his rifle and handed it to Billy.

Billy solemnly lifted the heavy gun. He aimed at the cloudless sky. The rifle went off and Billy staggered under the recoil. Whenever the rifle fired, it kicked back like a mule.

"Merry Christmas!" Billy cried.

Johnny cheered. Then his face fell. He was always too young to take a turn.

"I reckon it's time you tried it, too," Davy said. He loaded and held the long rifle, placing Johnny's hands on the gun. It would take two of Johnny's small fingers just to pull the trigger.

Boom! Johnny's ears rang with the blast. At the recoil, Johnny fell onto the seat of his pants. He stared up at the blue sky, not sure what had happened.

Everyone laughed, even Johnny.

"Merry Christmas!" he hollered.

CHAPTER 9

"Halt! Who goes there?" A sentry's voice called out.

"Just us. Davy and me," Georgie said. They had finally found Jackson's army deep in Alabama, in the heart of Creek country.

The camp was near the smoking ruins of a zigzag log wall. There were scorched gaps in the logs, like blacked-out teeth in a busted jaw. Davy wondered if he and Georgie had missed all the fighting.

The thin sentry who had challenged Davy and Georgie wore a tattered bandage on his head. The bandage was almost as grimy as his ragged uniform.

"Welcome back, boys," the sentry said and smiled.

"Reckon we better report to the general," Davy said. Georgie nodded.

"General Jackson and the cavalry are hunting Red Eagle," the sentry said. "They'll be back soon."

"Then who's in command?" Davy wondered.

"Major Norton," the sentry stated.

"If I'd have known that, I wouldn't have come back," Georgie grumbled.

"Well, come on! Let's get it over with," said Davy.

Norton sat on a bunk in his tent. His once-dapper uniform was stained, wrinkled, and torn. The gold braid on his shoulders was dull and smeared with mud. Rain drummed on the canvas and dripped steadily from cracks in the fabric overhead.

"I have to admit it, I'm glad to see you, Crockett," Norton confessed. "You, too, Russel. I'm at my wits' end. Most of my men are down with swamp fever. Afraid I've got a touch of it, too."

"You do look a little peaked, Major," Georgie observed.

Davy looked into the major's eyes. Something had changed. Hard experience had written a sad story on the man's face.

"Still chasing Red Eagle?" Davy asked.

"It's a question of who's chasing whom," Norton replied. "Every patrol I've sent out has failed to come back. He's outsmarted us at every turn.

"Three times we almost had him," Norton recalled. "At one village, Red Eagle was trapped. He escaped on horseback, leaping off a tall cliff right into the Alabama River! He is a brave man and a cunning warrior."

"What happened here?" Georgie wondered.

"Red Eagle and nearly a thousand of his warriors

made a last stand behind that log wall," Norton began. He shuddered at the memory.

"We started firing our cannon around ten in the morning. But the shots sank harmlessly into those thick logs.

"After two hours, Jackson stopped the barrage and ordered the 39th Infantry to charge. The soldiers ran to the wall and fired through the portholes. For a few minutes warriors and soldiers were shooting muzzle to muzzle.

"Major Montgomery of the 39th was the first man to mount the wall, and the first to die. Ensign Sam Houston was the next over." Norton continued. "Houston was hit in the thigh with an arrow, but he just kept fighting! The battle raged on all day. Near nightfall, we were forced to torch the fort with flaming arrows. It was horrible," Norton said. He buried his face in scarred and dirty hands.

"Just like Fort Mims," Davy said.

Norton nodded sadly. "But Red Eagle escaped again. He lay in the river shallows breathing through a hollow reed. After darkness fell, he swam away. The man is astounding! He doesn't have many warriors left. They can't hide forever in this infernal swamp. But neither can we!"

"Reckon we can help the army out, Georgie?" Davy asked.

"Looks like somebody's got to," Georgie replied.

"You fellas have held the dirty end of the stick long enough," Davy said. "Russel and I have rested up a mite. It's only fair we take a swing at it."

"No! No!" Norton protested. "That Indian has cost us enough lives already."

"Why Major! I didn't know you cared," Georgie teased.

"I've seen too much death," Norton said quietly. "You and I have had our differences, but I might as well admit you were right. The Indians are very intelligent and courageous, too. All they are is different, just as you and I are different. And I would rather not see you get killed. I refuse to let you two go out alone."

Davy looked at Georgie and said, "Looks like we'll have to start disobeying orders again."

It was a cold and cheerless day. The sky was a dull, gray slab above leafless cypress trees poking out from the cold, stagnant swamp. Davy and Georgie sloshed through water up to their hips.

"Great day for a swim," Georgie kidded. His sopping buckskins were heavy. He could barely lift his legs onto the muddy bank.

Davy pointed to a reed nest. Tiny green baby alligators crawled from pale, leathery eggs. They peeped and squeaked, blinking bulging eyes at the woodsmen.

"Kinda cute, aren't they?" Davy remarked.

"Not when they're grown up." Georgie shuddered. He hurried on.

They found moccasin prints pressed into the soft mud. Georgie stooped to get a closer look.

"Two days old, maybe more," he concluded.

"Moccasins just about worn out," Davy added. "They're heading around the lake."

"Suppose we scout both sides and meet at the other end?" Georgie suggested.

"If you see any fresh signs, whistle like a Tennessee thrush," Davy said.

They walked in opposite directions. Stands of dead trees stretched like skeleton hands reaching from the murky water. Flocks of birds swooped overhead, returning from their winter quarters. A fat alligator slid through rushes, its scaly tail whipping the new grass.

Georgie saw another footprint and called out like a thrush.

On the other side of the marsh, Davy started back toward his friend.

When he found yet another footprint, Georgie knew he was on the right track. He whistled again. This time a Red Stick's hand clamped over his mouth.

CHAPTER 10

Davy hurried toward the sound of Georgie's whistle. His keen ears had noticed that the whistle had ended abruptly. Something was wrong.

Davy held his rifle high above his head and waded chest-deep through the murky swamp. Through his worn moccasins, he felt his way among the stones and mud. He was concentrating on avoiding holes and buried roots. If he tripped and his rifle got soaked, he wouldn't be able to shoot.

With so much on his mind, it's no wonder Davy didn't notice the bulging eyes on a "log" drifting up behind him. Suddenly, out of the corner of his eye, Davy saw the "log" rush toward him with gaping jaws!

The big gator's pale pink mouth was ringed with jagged fangs. Its scaly tail whipped the water furiously. Davy smacked the gator's snout with the butt of his rifle.

The scaly varmint backed off, but Davy knew he'd

only bought a little extra time. He made for the bank as quickly as possible.

Davy easily found the trail his friend had been following. What he didn't find was Georgie. He figured Georgie had started following the trail, so he did the same.

Davy stopped at a jumble of footprints and flattened grass. Georgie's knife gleamed in the grass. Davy gripped his rifle. From the look of things someone must have grabbed Georgie and dragged him away. There was no time to lose!

Davy crept cautiously along. His keen eyes spotted broken twigs, mashed plants, and an occasional muddy moccasin print that marked Georgie's path. Soon he heard excited whoops and chanting among the moss-hung trees. Davy knew he was near the Red Stick camp.

He slipped closer. Through a veil of budding branches, Davy peered at the smoky campfire in a small clearing.

Red Eagle stood in the center of a chanting circle of warriors. Some wore soldier's coats and carried firearms won in war. The coats were pierced with bloody holes. The warriors were as patched and bloody as their clothing. Davy shook his head sadly, remembering Norton's account of the terrible battle.

Davy's heart sank as the crowd parted slightly and he caught sight of Georgie. He was tied to a stake. Georgie's ripped shirt hung in tatters at his waist. His arms were tied above his head with strong vines.

At his feet, a man with a white circle painted on his forehead kindled a small fire. A second Red Stick made torches of dry grass.

Red Eagle swaggered before Georgie. The Tastanagi demanded, "Where are the others? You did not come alone."

"I came alone," Georgie said calmly.

Just then, Davy stepped into the clearing. He held his rifle raised over his head. The Red Sticks turned and stared at him in amazement.

"Well make me a liar, why don't you?" Georgie said. "Only a fool like you would walk into a mess like this, Crockett."

The warriors looked to their Tastanagi. They were awed by the bravery of a lone man daring to walk into their camp.

"Red Eagle, hear me!" Davy called.

"Speak," the war chief responded.

"I'm not a soldier. I'm a settler," Davy began. "I live in a cabin like you do at home. I plant corn like you used to. I'm a hunter like you."

"You hunt *Indians*," Red Eagle spat.

"Only because you made war on us," Davy explained. "The White Stick chiefs know that war is no good.

"How many of your warriors have died?" Davy

asked. "How many of your women are crying for their men? How many of your younguns have no father?"

"You talk like a coward," Red Eagle said.

"I'm talking sense and you know it," Crockett countered. "You're brave, Red Eagle. And your warriors are brave. But in the end they're all going to die. You could go home in peace, if you'll listen to reason."

"I will fight to the last brave!"

"How about if you just fight me?" Davy offered.

Red Eagle laughed. "I cannot fight a duel of honor with you. Settlers have no honor."

"Weren't your father and grandfather honorable men?" Davy asked. "They were settlers. Your uncle, McGillivray, was a great warrior of the Revolution. Did he have no honor?"

Red Eagle frowned. He respected his own ancestors. When his own father had married a Creek woman, all had lived in harmony. But now settlers were stealing tribal lands. The days of peace were gone.

"Well, if you're scared—" Davy challenged.

Red Eagle snatched up his tomahawk. He tossed a war club and tomahawk to Davy. Each held the club in his left hand and the tomahawk in his right hand.

They went around in circles on the edge of the swamp, each searching for an opening. Red Eagle's warriors whooped and hollered. With a bloodcurdling shriek, Red Eagle lunged to make his first strike.

Davy just grinned.

Red Eagle was so surprised he stopped in his tracks.

Davy dropped his weapons and offered Red Eagle his empty hand.

The warriors stopped whooping. Everyone stared at Davy and Red Eagle. Georgie gasped. He wondered, What in tarnation is Crockett up to?

"Are you ready to listen to reason, Red Eagle?" Davy asked. Then he sat on a log just as naturally as if he were at a picnic.

"Turn my friend loose and lay down your arms," Davy began. "Join the other chiefs in a treaty. Do that and I promise that the government will let you go back and live in peace on your own land."

"We have no land," Red Eagle said. Then the Tastanagi sat on the log beside Davy. He continued talking in a low, angry voice and as he spoke, he moved closer to Davy. "Settlers have tricked our chiefs and cheated them out of tribal lands. They have lied. Land is a sacred thing, worth more than money or any marks on paper." Red Eagle moved even closer to Davy, who shifted down the log.

"We have always held dear the words the Great Tecumseh spoke to our people," Red Eagle continued. " 'Sell the country!' Tecumseh cried. 'Why not sell the air? The clouds? The seas as well as the earth? Did not the Great Spirit make them all for the use of his children?' "

Red Eagle moved nearer to Davy. Davy shifted once more. He was now on the end of the log.

"Now hold on there, Chief. I'm running out of log," he protested.

Red Eagle smiled. "Now you know how we feel. I went to war so we could keep enough room on our log. We have made treaties and they have been broken."

"Who broke them?" Davy wanted to know.

"Many years ago the Creeks made a treaty with the English," Red Eagle explained. "We gave them a little land on the coast. But the king of England gave the *whole territory* to settlers! He did not ask us. The king made many promises to keep us from fighting back. They were all false. Then, after the Revolution, the Americans refused to honor those early treaties. Years passed. We did not know what to do. We did not want war, but Tecumseh has convinced me that there is no other way."

"All you need is a new treaty," Davy said.

Red Eagle objected. "The king of England lied. How can I trust a new treaty?" he said. "What if this is also a lie?"

"Davy Crockett doesn't lie," Davy said. "I'll see you get a square deal, and here's my hand on it."

Red Eagle looked deep into Davy's eyes. He surveyed the clearing full of tired braves, then nodded gravely.

Davy and Red Eagle clasped hands.

"Mighty glad you patched things up," Georgie called from his stake. "Now would somebody untie me?"

CHAPTER 11

Davy and Georgie returned to the camp and hurried to tell General Jackson that Red Eagle had agreed to a treaty. Jackson did not believe them. And he was furious.

"You mean you let the war chief get away!" he demanded.

"It was more the other way around," Georgie said.

"Tarnation! I want that man hunted down and brought to me in chains!" Jackson thundered.

"Isn't it enough Red Eagle gave his word to stop the war?" Davy asked.

"How do we know he'll keep his word, Crockett? A man who'll slaughter innocent people won't think twice about breaking a promise. As far as I'm concerned, this war isn't over until Red Eagle surrenders!"

"With all due respect, General, we haven't been too good about keeping *our* promises to the Red Sticks.

They have plenty of reason to be suspicious of *us* keepin' *our* end of the deal."

"That doesn't concern me right now. I'll only believe Red Eagle when I see him standing before me."

"General," said Davy in a low voice, "I promised Red Eagle a square deal, and surrending to you wasn't part of it."

"You've made your opinions clear enough," retorted the general. "That will be all." And with that, Jackson turned and walked into his quarters.

Outside the general's tent, the army was packing up to go to New Orleans. The British had invaded Louisiana and were arming the Indian tribes there. Jackson was to lead the American defense.

In the bustle, no one noticed a tall, pale man in ragged deerskin breeches. He had entered the camp unarmed and on foot.

He stopped John Standingdeer.

"Where is Sharpknife?" the man asked in the Creek language.

Standingdeer led him to Jackson's tent.

"I am Bill Weatherford, Red Eagle," the man said. His green eyes were calm.

The general looked surprised, then scowled. "How dare you show yourself here? You murdered the women and children at Fort Mims!"

"I lost control of my young warriors," Red Eagle said, with a simple honesty.

Jackson was struck by the man's dignity.

"General Jackson, I am not afraid of you or of any man," the chief said. "But I can oppose you no longer. I am in your power."

Jackson shook his head.

"You are not in my power. I ordered you brought to me in chains. But you have come of your own free will," Jackson said. "If you wish to face me in battle, go and lead your warriors."

"That time has passed," Red Eagle replied. "Once I could have roused my warriors to battle. But I cannot raise the dead."

"Then why have you come here?" the general asked. "What do you want?"

"I ask nothing for myself. But my people need your help. Your soldiers have destroyed their fields, cabins, and corncribs, and now the women and children of the Creek nation are starving in the woods. I am asking you to send parties of your men to rescue them. General, these are innocent people who have harmed no one." Red Eagle paused, then added, "As for me, I am done fighting."

Jackson stared intently at Red Eagle. He could see that the chief's concern for his people was real and heartfelt. He saw, too, that Red Eagle was not much different from himself—they were both leaders of people for whom they cared deeply.

"I will save your people," said Jackson, finally. "We fought only to avenge our dead. We will live together in peace again."

Red Eagle shook hands with the frail, stern general. A moment later, he stepped out of the tent and was never seen again.

EPILOG

Davy Crockett is perhaps the most famous folk hero of the American frontier. He was born in 1786 and grew up in the rugged country of eastern Tennessee, where his father ran a small country inn. Business was never very good, and the family often relied on young Davy's hunting skills to put food on the table. But even in tough times, Davy had a knack for amusing himself and others with tall tales, a skill that was to later become part of the Crockett legend.

In 1806, Davy married Polly Finley, and they began to raise a family. As the frontier grew more crowded with settlers, Davy and Polly kept moving their family farther west. In 1813, Davy and his family moved for the last time, deep into western Tennessee.

Davy championed the rights of Native Americans in an era marked by great injustice toward Indian people. In 1813, he joined the army in an effort to negotiate an end to the Creek War. His efforts were successful, and in the process he earned the respect of both sides.

Davy returned from the war a hero and was so popular that

he was eventually elected to the United States Congress, where he served three terms. During that time, he helped draft a treaty that would have enabled the Indian people to keep their land. But in 1835, when Congress decided to break the treaty, and his efforts to save it failed, he decided not to run for reelection.

In 1836, Davy Crockett, along with his trusted companion Georgie Russel, joined a small band of brave American settlers under siege at the Alamo in San Antonio, Texas, which was then part of Mexico. The settlers fought long and valiantly in the name of freedom to defend themselves against the Mexican Army, but in the end their numbers were no match for the huge force amassed against them. The enemy soldiers finally overran the Alamo, killing every man, woman, and child within its walls. Davy Crockett died as he had lived—an American hero. And the phrase "Remember the Alamo!" lived on to inspire and unite the Americans in Texas, who eventually won their freedom from Mexico and brought Texas into the United States.